Enchanted Collar™ #3

Paradise Lost

by Robin Yang

Find color illustrations, previews, videos, toys, worksheets, and parenting tips on the Web at
www.EnchantedCollar.com

Like us on Facebook at
www.facebook.com/EnchantedCollar

Enchanted Collar™ books:

Here's what kids have say to Robin Yang, author of the Enchanted Collar™ series:

I love Earl. He is funny. I love Skipper too. He is so nice. I think he is shy.
— **Ava L., age 6, Connecticut**

I liked the book a lot, especially the pictures. I want to know what happens to Eli on his journey. I hope you write more soon so I can enjoy reading more about his story.
— **Brian G., age 7, New Jersey**

I liked this book as much as I like puppies, and I really love puppies! When I read Eli went out on his own and he couldn't read or write, I felt kind of sad and scared. Then I read about Earl, and I laughed because he was really funny!
— **Athena S., age 7, New York**

The stories were fun. I loved them. I keep telling my daddy I want a puppy; I tell him I wish I had a puppy like Eli.
— **Grace L., age 8, Connecticut**

I like the story and the characters. Earl is very funny, especially when he eats Eli's food. After all, he is a pig! When can I read the next book?
— **Jake R., age 9, Florida**

It's a very entertaining story. If I were Eli, I would have saved my money.
— **Sienna S., age 9, New York**

This was a really good book. I liked the words you used in the story. The words actually formed pictures in my head! I learned not to spend all of my money on one thing and to make my money to last a year or so. This story taught me a very good lesson.
— **Nathan X., age 11, Colorado**

This is a really great series of books! I like the fast-paced plot lines.
— **Taylor G., age 12, Connecticut**

I loved your story because it was cute. I could actually imagine what Eli, Earl, William, and all of the other characters looked like in my mind. I liked the fact that Eli never breaks his promises. Eli was very brave to accept such a dangerous quest and journey at such a young age. His story in Book 2 has taught me not to be greedy. I've learned that you should know how much something costs before you buy it and make sure you have enough money to pay. I am very eager to read the next book in the series.
— **Carol X., age 14, Colorado**

What teachers, parents, and financial experts say:

This book is an absolute gem. It entertains with a brisk tempo and reminds readers of the importance of financial literacy. Eli's journey is a page turner.
— **Kabir Seghal, investment banker and author of** *Walk in My Shoes* **and** *Jazzocracy*

I like the way Robin Yang's book weaves important financial precepts into an imaginative story that my children enjoyed reading. This establishes a basis for them to eventually learn the "mechanics" of money management.
— **Peter Lannigan, investment strategist, portfolio manager, and homeschooling father of two**

Robin Yang's book is a wonderful way to lead young children toward a successful financial future. Full of interesting and innovative ideas about budgeting, saving, banking, and investing, the Enchanted Collar™ series is a helpful and fun tool for teachers as well as students. Robin Yang should be congratulated for creating such an interesting method to teach kids about money.
— **Don Elliott, retired superintendent, Arkansas Public Schools**

Financial literacy, like literacy in general, should be acquired young. As a father as well as an economist, I look forward to my young son being able to read Robin Yang's imaginative and educational Enchanted Collar™ books.
— **Benn Steil, Ph.D., Director of International Economics for the Council on Foreign Relations and coauthor of**

Money, Markets and Sovereignty, **winner of the 2010 Hayek Book Prize**

What a great help this book is to all parents! The author does a fantastic job of telling stories to children and teaching them money management skills at the same time. The Enchanted Collar™ series is so fascinating that my children are eager to read more. The books teach them many good lessons about self-discipline, responsible spending, honesty, and hard work. These are the good values we would like our children to have, and the Enchanted Collar™ series does a marvelous job helping our kids learn these values. My children now have a better idea about banking and credit card use.
— **Melody Song, CPA, mother of two**

I loved how well-paced the stories were and how subtly the author was able to present a lesson on spending and saving. My daughters were completely enthralled with the first two books and can't wait for the rest of the series. My older daughter is more financially mindful and was surprised and frustrated that Eli and Earl didn't ask how much the meal would cost and budget more carefully. My younger daughter is our spendthrift so we are hoping the lessons will sink in!
— **Sonia O'Mara, artist, mother of two**

Paradise
Lost

For my mom and dad, who taught me priceless life lessons, and
for my big brother, who raised me and protected me

ISBN: 1466408847
ISBN-13: 9781466408845

Library of Congress Control Number: 2011918218
CreateSpace, North Charleston, South Carolina

TABLE OF CONTENTS

CHAPTER 1

A New Day

"Earl!" Eli rushed forward and held Earl in his arms. Earl did not answer. He had passed out.

Splash! Cold water poured over Earl and soaked Eli's shirt. Elda stood over them with one hand holding a pitcher and the other hand resting on her hip. Her mouth formed a smirk.

"What are you doing?" Eli roared and clenched his fist.

"Just trying to help." Elda shrugged.

"Where am I?" Earl jerked awake and shook water off his head. He sat up, rubbed his eyes, and looked around. "Wow, look at all that food!" He grinned from ear to ear. "We must be in heaven!" He lumbered toward the stoves and the kitchen counters, as if being reeled in by a fishing line.

"No!" Eli yanked him by the back of his collar. "We are not in heaven. We are in hell's kitchen!"

"Hey!" Elda scowled. "Don't offend my Papa's kitchen! Now get to work!" She stormed out.

"Work?" Earl rubbed his ears as if checking whether his hearing still functioned properly.

"Yes, work." Eli rolled up his sleeves. He grabbed a sponge off the sink and shoved it into Earl's hands. Then he picked up a brush and started rinsing dishes. After a few minutes, he looked over his shoulder to find Earl still standing there, petrified.

"Here." He pulled Earl by the arm to the sink. "I will show you."

It was past midnight before Eli and Earl finished washing all of the dishes. Eli looked up from the sink and stretched his back. The kitchen was empty except for Earl and him.

Everyone else had left. Earl yawned beside him. "What are we going to do now?"

"Well done, boys!" a deep voice boomed. It was Mr. Hills. He strode in with two little bundles underneath his arms. "How did you like your first night of work?"

"It was OK," Eli muttered.

"This is *really hard* work!" Earl declared with much drama and fanfare.

"I agree." Mr. Hills smiled. He threw down the bundles and patted Eli and Earl on their heads. "Next time, before you waste food, you might want to think about how hard you'll have to work to earn that food."

"Fine," Earl said, begrudgingly.

"Here, I've brought you sleeping bags." Mr. Hills unrolled the two bundles. "Sleep tight, boys! Tomorrow is a new day!"

"A new day in hell!" Earl grunted under his breath.

"What's that?" Mr. Hills asked.

Eli kicked Earl in the shin.

"Nothing!" they responded in unison and squeezed out smiles through gritted teeth.

"Good-night, boys!" Mr. Hills said as he walked out.

The kitchen became quiet. Eli looked around. Tiny blue flames danced on the gas stoves. He felt his eyelids grow heavy as lead. Before long, he was meandering in dreamland.

Eli wandered in a haze. He walked and walked but saw no sign of life except shadows of trees. In the distance, he spotted a little hut and a familiar figure standing in front of it.

Mom! Eli ran forward with his arms stretched out.

"Wake up, sleepy heads!" Eli opened his eyes. Bright rays of sun shone through the window. Eli shielded his eyes with his hands. The little hut and Mom had disappeared. Standing in front of him was a stout chimp chef. "It's almost noon! Time to get to work!"

Eli crawled out of his sleeping bag. Earl sat up and stretched his arms. A new day had begun.

Eli and Earl washed dishes, had breakfast, and then washed more dishes. Hours ticked by. Their fingertips started to wrinkle from being in the water so long. Richard, the lemur waiter, hurried in and unloaded another tray of dirty dishes into the sink.

"Oh, dear...," Earl moaned. He smashed down the sponge and huffed, "Those people out there have got to stop eating! Can't they see they've dirtied enough plates?"

"Ha!" Richard snickered. "Look who's talking!" Then he took on a more serious tone. "Be careful with what you wish for, boy! If those people out there stop eating, you and I will be out of a job. Then *we* can't afford anything to eat!"

"Whatever...," Earl muttered. He looked out the window and sighed. "I miss my good old days on the farm."

"Good old days?" Eli asked. "What was it like?

CHAPTER 2

Free Lunch

"Well," Earl began. He stood up straighter, and his eyes became dreamy. "Back in the good old days, I woke up in the morning, ate breakfast, took a nap, and it was lunch time. I ate lunch, took another nap, chatted with my spider friend, Charlene, and then it was dinnertime. I ate dinner, and then it was bedtime. There was always plenty of food and never this work junk!"

"It sounds kind of boring," Eli remarked.

"Boring?" Earl threw up his hands. "It was like a heaven on earth."

"If you like it so much," Eli asked, "why don't you go back to your pig farm?"

"Because…" Earl lowered his eyes. His dreamy look was gone. "Because I don't want to be taken to the slaughter-house again."

"That's right, boy!" a chef chimed in as he passed by and overheard their conversation. "There is no free lunch in this world!"

"No free lunch?" Eli asked the chef.

"That's right." The chef bent down and ruffled Eli's hair. "Everyone has to work, earn an honest living, and pay for his own lunch."

"But I didn't have to pay for my lunch when I was on the pig farm," Earl pouted. "My mom and dad did not pay for their lunches either."

"Ha!" the chef snorted. "You and your family paid a hefty price for your lunches, boy. You just didn't know it."

"Really?" Earl raised an eyebrow.

"Why do you think there are fences and locks on your pig farm?" The chef shoved his broad face so close to Earl's that their noses almost touched. "Why do you think your family was taken to a slaughterhouse?" The chef paused. Earl stared back at him but could not answer.

"The price of freedom, my boy, is honest work!" The chef thumped Earl's forehead as if trying to drill his words into Earl's brain. "Now get back to work!"

The price of freedom is honest work. Eli repeated the chef's words to himself. He was lost in thought.

Earl nudged him. "Hey, Eli, do you ever miss your days at home?"

"Yes," Eli answered. "I miss home a lot." He pictured the little hut and the familiar figure standing in front of it.

"Do you ever want to go back?" Earl asked.

Eli thought of his mom. In his mind, he saw her tearful eyes. Then something else came into focus. It was the money box. It was empty. It was staring at him like a giant, open mouth ready to swallow him whole.

"No." Eli hid his face as he turned on the water tap. "I don't want to go back."

"Really?" Earl gave him a baffled look. For the rest of the day, Eli refused to say a word.

Night fell and another morning rose. Several days passed. Eli and Earl slowly got used to working in the kitchen. They devised a procedure for washing dishes: Earl rinsed food off a plate and then handed it to Eli; Eli washed it clean with soap and then put it in bleach water for sterilization. When they were done with one batch of dishes, they both took dishes out of the bleach water and piled them up on the dish rack. Then they repeated the whole process.

Gradually, work no longer felt overwhelming. It became less tedious. It took on a rhythm. Eli started to enjoy his work. Earl still occasionally fell into nostalgia for his good old days when he didn't have to work.

One Friday morning, Eli noticed that everyone in the kitchen appeared happier than normal. People seemed to be stepping on springs. Hums and whistles of lighthearted melodies floated in the air.

"What's going on?" Eli asked a waiter zooming by.

"It's payday!" The waiter smiled as he waltzed away.

Psst! Eli whirled around. Earl was gesturing for him to come closer. It seemed something was bothering him. Eli put his right ear close to Earl. Earl cupped his hands over his mouth and whispered, "You won't believe what I just found out!"

"What's that?" Eli asked.

"Everyone else here is making far more money than we are!" Earl sputtered.

"So?" Eli didn't get what was the big deal.

"So? So?" Earl glared at Eli in disbelief. "You don't think it's unfair? We work as hard as everyone else, but we get paid the least. This is unfair! We are totally being exploited!"

"What is exploited?" Eli hated it when Earl threw big words at him.

"We are being taken advantage of!" Earl slammed one fist against his other palm. "We are being abused! This is outrageous! We should right the wrongs!"

Eli wiped Earl's spit off his right ear. He sort of got what Earl meant. No one liked to be abused, of course. But he did not quite understand how he and Earl were abused in particular. Everyone here was so friendly. Even Mr. Hills was courteous to them. They had plenty of food to eat, a roof over their heads at night, and a warm floor to sleep on.

"We should march into Mr. Hills' office and demand higher pay!" Earl went on with his rant. More spit flew onto Eli's right ear and the right side of his face. "We should show him we have dignity! We are not just a puppy and a piglet for him to kick around! We deserve to be treated fairly! We deserve equal pay!"

"OK, OK!" Eli wiped his face and ear. He had never seen Earl so furious, not even when Earl was being held hostage by the slaughterhouse bulldogs. *Being exploited must be worse than being taken to the slaughterhouse,* Eli reasoned. *Earl is right. We must right the wrongs!*

"Let's go!" Earl marched out. He waved his right arm forward like a general rallying his troops. "To Mr. Hills' office!"

CHAPTER
3

Equal Pay

Eli followed Earl out of the kitchen and through the corridor toward Mr. Hills' office. The office door was ajar. Eli could hear two people talking.

"Still no one has come to claim those two?" It was Mr. Hills' voice.

"No, boss," said Lance, the black German shepherd. "I've put up notices all over town. No one has come. It has been a week. Should I take down the notices?"

"No, let's leave them up a little longer and see what happens," Mr. Hills said.

Bam! Earl slammed the door open and charged in with Eli in tow. The doorknob hit the wall behind the door and made a dent.

"Can I help you boys?" Mr. Hills asked with raised eyebrows as he swiveled his chair to face Earl. Lance cracked his knuckles. He did not wear his usual dark sunglasses. His big brown eyes bore into Eli and Earl with flaming anger.

"Uh…," Earl stammered. "We… uh…"

"We think we are being exploited." Eli stepped forward. "We demand equal pay."

"Really?" Mr. Hills said bemusedly. "Exploited?"

Eli glanced uneasily at Earl. He was not sure if he had pronounced the word "exploited" right. He hoped Earl would help, but Earl just stood there like an open-mouthed statue.

"Yes," Eli quavered. Out of the corner of his left eye, he saw Lance step forward, but Mr. Hills gestured for him to stand back. Eli tried to calm the flutter in his stomach and maintain a steady voice. "We've heard everyone else here makes far more money than we do. We demand equal pay."

"But, my child," Mr. Hills began, biting his lip to suppress a chuckle, "you are not doing the same work as everyone else. How do you expect me to give you equal pay?"

"But we work just as hard as the others!" Eli said angrily. He felt deeply insulted. How could Mr. Hills say he was not doing work equal to the others?

"I appreciate your hard work," Mr. Hills replied, leaning forward, "but you job does not require the skill of a chef or a waiter."

"But I can be a chef or a waiter, too," Eli protested. "You just did not offer me the job!"

"Can you read and write?" Mr. Hills asked. "Can you do math?"

"No." Eli was confused. What did reading, writing, and math have to do with cooking or waiting tables?

"If you can't read and do math," Mr. Hills asked, "how can you read customers' orders and follow food recipes? How can you calculate the right amount of ingredients when you cook?"

I have to know how to read and do math just to be a cook? Eli thought. He felt a little deflated.

"If you can't do math," Mr. Hills continued, "how would you know how much money the customers owe you? How would you make sure you gave them the right amount of change?"

Eli's shoulders drooped. He wished he knew how to read and do math like Earl. *Earl!* Eli piped up, "Earl knows how to read and do math! Why don't you let him be a waiter?"

Hearing his name, Earl was jolted out of his trance. "Yeah… I should be paid just as much as a waiter!"

"You?" Mr. Hills assessed Earl as if seeing him for the first time. Then he stood up. "OK, let's see if you can do a waiter's job then. Follow me."

Eli and Earl followed Mr. Hills to a room next door. Eli saw a treadmill and some dumbbells lying on the floor. It was Mr. Hills' private gym. He picked up two dumbbells and handed them to Earl. Earl took them, almost buckling under their weight.

"Are you OK, boy?" Mr. Hills asked Earl while leaning against the tread-mill. "Those are only eight-pounders."

"Sure." Earl winced.

"Great!" Mr. Hills patted the tread-mill handle. "Hop on!"

Earl trudged onto the treadmill. Mr. Hills punched a few buttons on its panel. The belt started to move. Earl stepped forward. At first, he managed to stay in sync with the pace of the belt. But as the belt accelerated, Earl had to pick up his steps. Sweat started to seep through his shirt. His face turned red. His breaths became shorter. He was having trouble keeping up.

Flop! Earl fell off the treadmill. *Thump! Thump!* The two dumbbells rolled out of his hands. Earl lay on his stomach, panting.

"Four minutes and thirty seconds!" Mr. Hills read his watch. He knelt down on one knee beside Earl. "My boy, if you a waiter, you'll have to carry a tray of food heavier than these dumbbells and hustle back and forth all day long. Do you still want to be a waiter?"

No answer came. Earl shook his head on the floor weakly. He did not even bother to stand up.

"Take your time to catch your breath." Mr. Hills stood up. "I will be in my office if you have any more questions." He strolled away.

Eli rolled Earl over onto his back. "Earl," Eli asked in earnest, "will you teach me how to read, write, and do math?"

"OK, if you will help me up first," Earl answered.

Eli extended his hand. Earl took it.

CHAPTER
4

Number Seventy-Eight

When Eli and Earl slogged back into the kitchen, they found Elda waiting beside the sink.

"Good news, boys!" Elda announced happily. "Some people have come to claim you two."

"Mom?" Eli's eyes lit up. He wanted to see her right away.

"Mom?" Elda raised an eyebrow. "Didn't you say your parents died?"

"Oh…" Eli lowered his head. He did not know how to backpedal out of this one.

Elda crossed her arms. "As far as I can tell, those people are no moms. They are both male bulldogs. They have come to claim Earl, and they want you as well."

"Oh, no!" Earl inhaled. The color vanished from his cheeks. "They must be the slaughterhouse bulldogs!" He rushed forward and grasped Elda's arm. "You've got to save me!"

"Slaughterhouse?" Elda was mystified.

Earl explained everything. Elda listened intently. Her eyebrows were knitted into a tight knot. When Earl finished, she said, "Stay here, both of you. I will take care of those bulldogs."

As he watched Elda disappear through the kitchen doorway, Eli whispered to Earl, "You wait here. I want to see what she's up to." He crept after Elda. He did not quite trust her.

In the hallway, Elda ran into Lance. "Come with me, Lance," she ordered.

"Yes, Miss Elda."

They stepped into the front lobby. Eli hid behind a ficus tree in the hallway and peered out. The two bulldogs paced impatiently. One wore a bandage on his right hand. The other wore a bandage around his neck.

"Gentlemen," Elda said in a sweet and innocent voice, "I am so sorry. Our piglet and puppy said they don't know you. They said they have no bulldog relatives in their families."

"They are lying!" cried one bulldog as he hammered his fist on the reception desk. A pen jumped up and fell onto the ground.

"OK," Elda said, unperturbed, "if you are such caring uncles to those boys, tell me something: What are their names?"

"What are their names?" one bulldog asked the other.

"How would I know?" the other bull-dog shot back. "All I know is we've lost pig number seventy-eight."

"I am so sorry, gentlemen." Elda smiled. "No one here is called Number Seventy-eight. Maybe you should check some other places? Lance, please show these gentlemen out."

"Wait…" The bulldogs stalked over but bounced off Lance's stretched arms.

"The door is that way," Lance said curtly. "Good day, gentlemen."

The two bulldogs exchanged looks of frustration but decided not to try their chances. They turned on their heels and stormed out.

Phew! Eli let out a sign of relief. He was thankful for Elda's quick wit and Lance's strength.

As Eli ran back to the kitchen to deliver the good news to Earl, he felt something heavy in his heart. *Where is Mom? If the bulldogs have seen the notice about lost children, shouldn't Mom have seen it as well? Why doesn't she come? Doesn't she miss him? Doesn't she love him anymore?*

Earl was pacing in front of the kitchen sink nervously. Hearing Eli's footsteps, he cast an expectant look and noticed Eli's long face. He sank to his knees, whining, "Oh, no, I am going to die."

"No, no!" Eli hurried over. "Everything is fine now. Elda told the bulldogs to get lost. Lance hurried them out the door. We are safe now."

"Yeeeaaahhh!" Earl leaped with joy. He danced around but then realized Eli did not join him. "What's wrong?" Earl asked.

"Why hasn't my mom come?" Eli sat down on the floor, hugged his knees to his chest, and buried his face. "I miss her."

Earl scratched his head and said, "Well, why don't you go visit her? I will cover for you."

"You will?" Eli looked up. A smile turned up the corners of his mouth while tears still ran down his cheeks.

"Sure!" Earl squared his shoulders. "That's what friends are for. I can wash the dishes by myself."

"Thanks!" Eli jumped to his feet and was ready to run out the door.

"Wait!" Earl stopped him. "Wait for tomorrow. Those bulldogs may still be lurking around. Wait until the coast is clear before you go."

Eli counted the minutes and seconds for the day to pass. That night, he tossed and turned. As soon as the first ray of daylight shone through the window, Eli got up. Earl was still snoring loudly. Eli tiptoed out the door and started for home.

CHAPTER 5

Home, Sweet Home

Eli ran through the empty city streets, which were covered with dew. He scurried on the forest trail, which glittered in the sun. He sprang across the valley creek, singing in the dusk. He ran and ran and ran. He was going to see Mom soon!

When the sun was about to sink behind the west mountain, Eli saw the familiar shapes of giant magnolia trees. Smoke rose from beneath their canopy. *Mom must be cooking dinner now,* Eli thought. He quickened his steps. Then he remembered something. His steps slowed to a trot. What was he going to tell Mom? How would he explain the delay in his search for the cure?

As he plodded toward his hut, Eli saw smoke billowing into the sky. *What's going on?* He felt his heart jump to his throat. *That smoke is too thick to be from a cooking fire,* he thought uneasily. Eli raced forward.

In the place where his hut used to be, he saw smoke hanging over collapsed mud walls. The straw roof was completely gone.

"Mom!" Eli roared at the top of his lungs. He darted toward the ruins like an arrow from a bow. There was no answer. Other than the occasional sparks crackling in the ruins, there was dead silence all around.

Eli jumped over the crumpled mud walls. He searched frantically. Where was Mom? What had happened to his home? Who had started the fire? He rummaged around in the living room but saw nothing other than empty pots and pans scattered around. He searched what used to be Mom's bedroom but found nothing except blackened wood posts and piles of ashes.

Eli collapsed onto the ground. Then something glittering in the ashes caught his eye. He looked closer. Something metallic was half buried beneath the burned wood. He scooped away the ashes and picked up a round disk. It was a copper belt buckle engraved with a coyote.

"The coyotes!" Eli clenched the belt buckle in his fist. He bolted out of the ruins into the forest. He wanted to track down the coyote guards, the coyote king, and whoever had burned down his hut. He wanted an eye for an eye, a tooth for a tooth.

Eli charged east but saw no sign of the coyotes. He stormed west but found no trace. He dashed north—still nothing. He thrust south. This time, he saw a shadowy figure sitting under a tree. Eli charged with all his might at the shadow. As he got closer, however, he recognized a familiar face with a large scar.

"William!" Eli flew into the big wolf's open arms. Tears streamed down his face. "Oh, William! What have they done to my home? What have they done to my mom?"

"Shh." William held Eli close to his chest. "It's OK. Everything will be alright. Your mom is in a safe place."

"Safe place?" Eli's eyes twinkled. "Where?"

"It's a secret." William stroked Eli's hair. "For her safety, it's better no one knows where she is. A few days after you left, I saw the two coyote guards hanging around your house at night. I alerted your mom. She moved to a safe place far away. I kept your house the same as normal and pretended that your mom was still home every night. One night the coyote guards set your house on fire."

"The coyotes!" Eli's eyes were flaming. He curled up his fist and shouted, "William, let's track down those coyote guards and that evil coyote king!"

"OK," William agreed but did not move. "What are we going to do if we find them?"

"We will avenge my father's death!" Eli slammed the coyote belt buckle onto the ground. "We will kill them!"

William picked up the belt buckle, studied it for a second, and then handed it back to Eli. "Right now we are two people against the coyote king's entire army. Do you think we will be able to kill them? Or do you think

49

we'll just walk into their trap and be killed?"

Eli could not answer. William dusted the wood ash gently off Eli's shoulders. He tilted Eli's chin upward so their eyes could meet. "Remember, never fight force with force." William emphasized every syllable. "Even if you win the battle, you will still get hurt."

"Then how are we going to fight them?" Eli demanded.

"We will fight them with our brains, wits, and patience," William answered. "Once you find the cure, the coyote king's reign will crumble to the ground on its own. When the wolf citizens regain their sanity, they will rise together and overthrow the coyote king. He will be held accountable for all of the evil he has done."

"Yes!" Eli thrust his fist into the air.

"But if we seek revenge now," William continued, "we will have to fight not only the coyote king and his army, but the mad wolf citizens as well."

"Oh..." Eli's fist went limp. His shoulders slouched. What William said made sense: Find the cure first, and the coyote king's regime would collapse on its own. Oh, the cure... Eli reached for his collar. It was still safe around his neck.

William smiled warmly at him. "That's a mighty powerful collar you've got there. Tell me, Eli, why are you back here? Have you found the cure already?"

"No." Eli could barely hear his own voice. Reluctantly, he told William the truth. He recounted his whole experience since he had left home. When he finished, William did not say anything but scrutinized him with curious eyes. Eli met his gaze and asked, "What do you think I should do now?"

CHAPTER 6

Big Success, Small Actions

William did not answer. He thought for a moment and then asked in return, "What do you think your father would do?"

"I am not sure," Eli said to his shoes.

"I think he would go back to that restaurant," William said.

"Really?" Eli looked up in surprise.

"Yes," William said firmly. "He would go back to that restaurant to pay his debt. He would try to be the best dish-washing boy in the world. Not only that—when he wasn't busy washing dishes, he would learn as much as he could."

"Learn about what?" Eli could not understand William's excitement.

"He would learn from the chefs how to cook," William answered enthusias-tically. "He would learn from the wait-ers how to make customers happy. He would learn from the cougar girl how to do math. He would learn from the cougar man how to run a restaurant."

"But my father was the wolf king!" Eli argued. "Why should a king bother to cook, serve customers, or do math? He ran a kingdom, not a restaurant!"

"But, my boy," William answered, "if he did not know how to cook and feed himself, how would he know how to feed his people? If he did not know how to make customers happy, how could he make his citizens happy? If he did not know how to do math, how could he make sure not to overspend his kingdom's money? If he couldn't even run a restaurant, how could he run a kingdom that's ten thousand times bigger than a restaurant?"

Eli fell silent. He could not believe he had to learn all those things to be a king. They seemed so boring! He had imagined being a king would be grand and fun, like the games he played when he lived in the village. Now he realized running a kingdom would be a complex and difficult task.

"Big success starts with small actions," William said, helping Eli to his feet. "A journey of a thousand miles starts with one step. Remember, whatever you do, do your best. Learn something from everyone you meet. One day, you will realize that everything you have learned will benefit you for the rest of your life."

Eli nodded in agreement. "I will remember. I will go back to the restaurant. But…" He searched William's eyes. "I just want to see Mom one more time before I go back."

William's eyes met Eli's. "If you visit her now, you may accidentally lead the coyote guards to her hiding place. For her safety and yours, it's better for you not to see her now. If you miss her, then write to her."

"Write her…," Eli repeated. He patted his knapsack and felt the notepad and the pencil set inside. He remembered what mom had said about writing her letters once he had learned how to read and write.

"But how can she get my letters if I don't know where she lives?" Eli asked.

"Through a messenger." William put his thumb and index finger in his mouth and whistled softly three times. A bird flew over and landed on William's left shoulder. She had a black head, black eyes, a yellow beak, a gray back, and a red chest. She cocked her head to one side and eyed Eli with curiosity.

William took the bird into his palm and handed her to Eli. "Meet Robin, your messenger. She will deliver your letters to your mom."

Eli stroked Robin's head and back. Her feathers felt soft and smooth.

Robin cooed gently, as if saying, "Nice to meet you!"

"Now let's practice your signal to call Robin over." William showed Eli how to whistle. Robin danced between Eli and William at their whistles. When William made sure Eli had mastered the trick, he tossed Robin up into the air. She flapped her wings, circled above their heads three times, and then flew away.

Eli bid good-bye to William and started on his way back to the restaurant. It was close to noon when he got there. When Earl saw Eli walk into the kitchen, he hollered, "Thank goodness, you are back! My back is about to break, doing two people's work!"

Eli picked up a sponge and joined Earl at the sink.

"How is your mom?" Earl asked.

"I didn't see her." Eli lowered his head. He told Earl everything.

Earl sighed. "I am so sorry, Eli."

"It's OK." Eli tried to inject a light tone into his voice. "When we finish work tonight, will you show me how to write? I want to write Mom a letter right away."

"You've got it!" Earl answered.

From that day on, Eli worked more energetically than ever before. Every night, he learned to read and write.

When there were few dishes to wash, he helped the chefs clean work stations, wash vegetables, and marinate meat. When he asked the chefs about cooking, they gladly answered his questions. They showed him how to read recipes, measure ingredients, and boil, fry, sauté, bake, and grill. They even let Eli experiment with new dishes on his own.

When the kitchen was not busy, Eli helped waiters clean tables, mop floors, fold napkins, and refill water pitchers. When he asked them about waiting on customers, they offered up all sorts of stories and tips. They showed him how to ask questions to figure out what customers want, how to make them feel special, how to bring smiles to their faces, and how to encourage them to come back again.

Eli felt a whole new world unfolding in front of him. He realized everyone had something to teach him. He saw an opportunity to learn everywhere he went. He felt like a gold miner, picking up nuggets of valuable skills. He enjoyed learning everything, except one thing—math.

CHAPTER 7

Food for Math

For several nights, Eli had been trying to get Earl to show him how to do multiplication and division. He wanted to figure out how Elda had decided that both of them needed to work sixteen and a half days to pay back Mr. Hills. Unfortunately, Earl got a different answer every time he did the math.

Apparently, he was lousy with numbers but didn't want to admit it.

One night, after everyone else had left and Earl had gone to sleep, Eli stayed up, working on his math problem. He tried to rework the math several times but kept getting stuck on the multiplication.

"What are you doing?" a girl's voice asked.

Eli looked up to see Elda. His face turned crimson. He tried to cover his worksheet with his body. He did not want Elda to think he was dumb, but it was too late. Elda snatched away his worksheet.

"Give it back!" Eli demanded.

"I will, in a minute." Elda studied the worksheet carefully. "Oh, I see. You've got the multiplication of percentages wrong. Here, I will show you."

Elda sat down beside Eli and picked up his pencil. She showed him step by step how to do multiplication and division. Her way of doing math was so much clearer than Earl's. Finally, they reached the conclusion that Eli had been looking for: sixteen and a half days. It was crystal clear to Eli now how math should be done properly.

"Thank you," Eli said sheepishly. "Will you be my math teacher?"

Elda tilted her chin up. "Why should I?"

Eli rolled his eyes. This girl never made anything easy for him! He racked his brain for something Elda might like. "If you teach me math," he offered, "I will cook you special dishes."

"You?" Elda wrinkled her nose. "You know how to cook?"

"Yep!" Eli flushed with pride. "I've learned. Wait here." He ran to the kitchen. A minute later, he came back with a plate. "I just cooked this tonight. Try it." He handed Elda a fork.

She dipped the fork into the dish with suspicion and took a small bite. As she chewed, her face glowed. "Wow, this is delicious! What's it called?"

"I don't have a name for it." Eli scratched his head. "I am not even sure what cooking style this is. The chefs here keep different spices of various cooking styles on separate racks. I just mixed and matched a bunch of spices from different racks into this vegetable dish."

"This is the best fusion veggie dish I have ever had," Elda gushed.

"What is fusion?" Eli asked.

"Fusion means mixing different features of different cuisines together," Elda explained. "We will call it the Eli dish."

"But I can cook many more dishes, not just this one," Eli offered. "How about this? If you give me a math lesson every night, I will cook you a different dish every day."

"Deal!" Elda jumped at the offer. They shook hands and laughed.

Eli felt very happy. He started to like Elda. She was not the spoiled brat he had imagined she was. He was so excited about finally finding a good math teacher that he did not notice two shadows float past the window.

That night, Eli slept deeply. He had been working nonstop since morning, and he was exhausted. The warm summer breeze blew through the open window. In the distance, crickets sang in a symphonic choir.

In his dreams, Eli saw Mom. He showed her his math work. She nodded approvingly. He read a book aloud to her. She smiled graciously. Eli was wrapped in joy. He wanted Mom to hug him and tell him she was proud of him. But when he stepped forward, smoke rose from underneath Mom. Soon, the smoke became so thick that it engulfed her.

"Mom!" Eli yelled. He woke up and realized something strange was going on in the kitchen.

CHAPTER
8

Fire!

In the moonlight, Earl was dangling from the arms of a bulldog. He kicked, but his feet could not touch the floor. He made mumbling noises, but no scream came. The bulldog's hand covered his mouth.

Before Eli could rescue Earl, the other bulldog grabbed him by his waist and hauled him up into the air. Eli wriggled and kicked. Then he twisted backward and slammed his neck against the bulldog's face.

"Ahh!" With a shriek of pain, the bulldog dropped Eli onto the floor and covered his eyes. Eli's collar had spiked up and blinded him. Eli bolted for the bulldog holding Earl.

"Freeze!" the bulldog yelled, holding Earl above the deep fryer, "or I will drop him!" Bubbles puffed in the fryer.

Eli stopped dead in his tracks.

"Give me your collar!" the bulldog ordered.

Eli did not move. He hesitated.

"Or your friend will become fried pork!" the bulldog threatened.

Eli slowly removed his collar. He held the bulldog's eyes. "Put him on the floor first. Then I will give you my collar."

"You give me your collar first!" the bulldog barked.

"No." Eli held his ground. "If I give you my collar first, you will still kill Earl. Put him down first. Then your hands will be free to take my collar."

The bulldog dumped Earl onto the floor and charged at Eli. Before he could reach Eli, however, he doubled over and held his right leg, writhing in pain. Earl had bitten his leg. Eli sprang forward and hit the bulldog's left knee with his spiked collar. The bulldog rolled on the floor, holding both of his legs.

Crash! Ding! Bam! Eli spun around. The other bulldog was stumbling across the room, his hands stretched out in front of him. He knocked pots and pans to the floor, making loud, clattering noises. The bulldog fumbled and seized a large rolling pin off the counter. He swung it aimlessly, hoping to hit Eli or Earl. Instead, the rolling pin struck the fryer and knocked it over. Oil splashed over the stove. A blaze shot up to the ceiling.

Eli and Earl dashed to the stove to put out the fire. Just then, two more shadows jumped through the window into the kitchen.

"No one moves!" one shadow growled. It was the one-eyed coyote guard, carrying a mace. Beside him stood the half-eared coyote guard, carrying a sword.

In the light of the blazing fire, Eli saw the look of murder in their eyes. He froze. Earl stood speechless beside him.

The one-eyed coyote kicked the injured bulldog on the floor. "Take your useless pal and get out of my way!"

The crippled bulldog hobbled to his feet, grabbed the blind bulldog by the arm, and scrambled out the door.

The half-eared coyote aimed his sword at Eli. "Give me your collar."

Eli held out his collar and waited. He was about four feet away from the coyote guards. His fingers gripped the collar tightly.

"No one moves!" a deep voice rumbled.

Eli craned his neck toward the voice. It was Mr. Hills and Lance!

The half-eared coyote guard took his eyes off Eli and swung his sword at Mr. Hills. Mr. Hills ducked to the left, dodged the sword blow, and delivered a powerful jab to the coyote's chin. The coyote stumbled backward. His sword flew out his hand and hit the spice rack on its way down. Dry herbs splattered over the stove. More flames shot up.

"You dirty old cat!" The one-eyed coyote charged violently toward Mr. Hills. Lance leaped high into the air and kicked him in the head. The one-eyed coyote staggered and dropped his mace.

The half-eared coyote rushed over and helped him to his feet, and they both escaped through the window.

Before Lance could chase after them, Mr. Hills stopped him and pointed at the fire. They all dashed for the kitchen sink. Lance turned on the tap. Eli grabbed a pot. Earl picked up a pan. Mr. Hills filled a bucket with water. He flung water over the blazing kitchen counter.

Whoosh! Flames spread from the counter to the floor. *What's going on?* Eli's eyes widened. The fire seemed to be burning the water!

"Oil fire, boss!" Lance yelled. "We can't fight it with water! We need to get out of here."

"Come on, boys!" Mr. Hills waved at Eli and Earl. "Let's go!"

"My books!" Earl ran toward his sleeping bag in a corner.

"My knapsack!" Eli followed him. He did not want to lose the last birthday gift Mom had given him.

Just as Eli grasped his knapsack and Earl got hold of his backpack, two powerful hands lifted them off the ground. Mr. Hills tucked them underneath his arms and ran out of the kitchen. A loud clanging noise followed them. One of the roof beams had caught on fire and caved in.

CHAPTER 9

Ruby Heart

Mr. Hills put Eli and Earl down in the empty yard outside the restaurant. They turned around to see the whole building engulfed in flames. Wooden tables and chairs crackled as they burned.

"Papa!" Elda came running, Lance on her heels. She flew into Mr. Hills' arms. "Thank goodness, you are OK!"

A slight feeling of envy rose in Eli as he watched Mr. Hills wrap his arms around Elda. He wished his mom was holding him at that very moment.

"What happened, Papa?" Elda asked.

Mr. Hills turned to Eli. "I presume those two bulldogs must be after Earl. Elda told me a few days ago they came to claim him. But who are those coyotes, and why are they after you?"

Eli rubbed the collar around his neck. He couldn't hide anything from Mr. Hills, not after he had saved his life. With a heavy heart, he told Mr. Hills, Lance, and Elda about his collar and about Mom, Dad, William, the coyote king, and the coyote guards.

Mr. Hills stared at him in disbelief. "You are the wolf prince?"

"Yes," Eli admitted.

Mr. Hills extended an open hand to his daughter. "Elda, give me your necklace."

Elda looked perplexed but followed her father's order nonetheless. She took off her necklace and gave it to Mr. Hills.

Mr. Hills twisted the heart shape, broke out a ruby, and handed it Eli. "Put this ruby in your collar."

"But, Papa," Elda protested, "it's mine!"

"No." Mr. Hills shook his head. "It was never yours. We were safekeeping this ruby at the wolf king's request. Now its rightful owner is here."

"You knew my father?" Eli was shocked.

"Yes," Mr. Hills said. "I was a cougar diplomat to your father's kingdom. When the coyote took over your father's throne, I resigned my post in disgust. I decided to retire early and opened this restaurant. A few months after I left, your father came to me and gave me this ruby. He asked me to keep it safe until the day you came to claim it."

Eli inserted the ruby into the little wolf medallion in his collar. A bright red light shone from the little wolf's heart. Everyone gasped. Eli ran his fingers over the little wolf. The red light dimmed and then went out.

He put the collar back around his neck and faced Mr. Hills. "Thank you, sir. I am so sorry about your restaurant. It's all my fault. How can I ever pay you back for your loss?"

"Don't worry about it, my boy!" Mr. Hills slapped Eli's back good-naturedly. "Go on your journey, and become a king!"

Eli remained concerned. "But you've just lost everything you own. What are you going to do now?"

"I will build another restaurant, of course!" Mr. Hills beamed with confidence. He did not seem to be a bit worried. "A bigger one and a better one! They can burn down my restaurant, but they can't take away the knowledge in my head. With this"—he tapped his temple—"and these"—he held out his hands—"I can build another restaurant!"

"And I will help you, Papa!" Elda chimed in.

"Yes!" Mr. Hills smiled broadly and wrapped his arm around her shoulder. "With my little math whiz here, we will be able to hit the ground running in no time. Before you know it, our customers will be lined up in our lobby again, waiting for a table!"

"But I still owe you money," Eli insisted. "We have not worked for sixteen and a half days yet."

"I will put that on your tab," Mr. Hills chuckled. "You can pay me back after you become a king."

"I sure will!" Eli said brightly. He turned to Elda and added, "When I become a king, I will buy you a bigger ruby necklace."

"Promise?" Elda tilted her head.

"Promise!" Eli hooked his little finger with Elda's.

"I am afraid you children have to sleep in the open air tonight," Mr. Hills said. "Lance and I will stand guard. If those coyotes and bulldogs dare to show up again, we will kick them into the clouds!" Everyone roared with laughter.

Mr. Hills sat down under the starry sky. Lance stood beside them and kept a watchful eye around the perimeter of the yard. Elda, Eli, and Earl huddled together and used Mr. Hills' legs as pillows. They slept peacefully through the night.

The next morning, Eli rose before Earl and Elda woke up. He murmured the magic words into his collar, which shone a bright path in front of him. Mr. Hills and Lance nodded approvingly at him. Eli memorized the direction and said the magic words again. The collar's light went out.

Eli woke up Earl. Together they bowed deeply to Mr. Hills and Lance, and then they walked toward the rising sun.

Step by step, the road before them gradually changed from a paved city street to a narrow dirt path and then to a winding trail covered with dry leaves. Eli and Earl traveled during the day and made camp at night. They ate wild fruit and mushrooms. They drank clear creek water. As they trekked through the mountains, Earl helped Eli memorize arithmetic tables.

"One plus one is two. One plus two is three...," Eli recited. Birds flapped their wings as if applauding. Eli kept going. "Seven minus six is one. Seven minus five is two...Two times three is six. Two times four is eight..."

One day, they passed through a dense forest. Earl quizzed Eli as they walked side by side on the forest trail. "What is ten divided by five?"

"Two!" Eli answered without hesitation.

"Help!" A faint cry rippled through the wind in the distance. "Someone help me!"

Eli and Earl looked at each other in surprise and then bolted toward the crying voice.

Don't miss the next
Enchanted Collar™ book,
in which Eli meets a new friend, Skipper, and
escapes from the flying arrows of a mad hunter!

Enchanted Collar™ #4

Squirrel Pot Pie

Want more than just the stories? Visit the *Enchanted Collar*™ website at www.EnchantedCollar.com Find illustrations in full vivid color! Get exciting sneak previews of the next book! Watch videos and enjoy other fun activities! And much more!

Connect with the author and other *Enchanted Collar*™ fans on FaceBook at www.facebook.com/EnchantedCollar

Robin Y. Yang, MBA, CFA

is the author of the *Enchanted Collar*™ and *Economic Fairy Tales*™ series of books. She has been an investment analyst for thirteen years, during which she has published extensive investment research reports, been quoted in various publications, and delivered speeches at investment conferences.

After experiencing two major American financial crises, she started teaching children the basics of finance as a Junior Achievement volunteer. In 2011, she started writing the Enchanted Collar™ series and the Economic Fairy Tales™ series in her spare time to promote financial literacy among children and young adults.

Despite the fact that Ms. Yang used to wear a business suit and analyze dollars and cents on Wall Street, she remains a child at heart. Her favorite movies are animations. Wherever she travels, she makes a point to visit petting zoos, her favorite destinations. She lives and works in New York City.

Made in the USA
Lexington, KY
27 February 2012